Plucky Duck in
THE SUMMER JOB

This Tiny Toon Adventures Book is published by Longmeadow Press,
in association with Sammis Publishing.
Distributed by Book Sales, Inc., 110 Enterprise Ave.,
Secaucus, NJ 07904

With special thanks to

Guy Gilchrist • Gill Fox • Tom Brenner • Marie Gilchrist
Brad Gilchrist • Jim Bresnahan • Rich Montesanto • John Cacanindin
Ron Venancio • Norma Rivera • Allan Mogel • Gary A. Lewis

Printed in the United States of America
0 9 8 7 6 5 4 3 2 1

Plucky Duck in
THE SUMMER JOB

written by Gary A. Lewis

Illustrated by
The *Guy Gilchrist* Studios

It was summertime, and Plucky Duck and his friends were out of school. Buster Bunny, Babs Bunny, Hamton, and the rest of the gang were at the beach every day. That's where Plucky had thought he'd be, too.

But Plucky had a little problem.

Plucky had spent all of his allowance that year on comic books. He had no money left at all.

And there was something he wanted more than anything—a new stereo system. He had seen just the one in the local Cousin Eddie's Electronics Emporium.

So Plucky decided he needed a summer job.

Plucky's first stop was the office of the local paper, *The Acme Acres News*.
There he met the editor-in-chief, Mr. "Scoop" Johnson.
"I've got room for a paper boy, if you want the job," Mr. Johnson told him.

zip!

"I sure do!" said Plucky Duck. "I've got a bicycle and everything. When do I start?"

"How about tomorrow morning?" asked Mr. Johnson. He and Plucky shook hands. Then Plucky raced out the door to tell his friends.

Plucky got to work bright and early the next day. He wanted to deliver all the papers before nine o'clock, so that he could meet Buster Bunny and the gang at the beach.

He tossed the first paper up on the porch of Mr. McGillicuddy. It landed right on a rocking chair.

Not bad! thought Plucky.

He tossed the second paper right through the window of Mrs. Gilhooley's house. The only problem was, the window wasn't open.

"Your first day's salary should pay for my broken window," Mrs. Gilhooley told Plucky.

"I have a feeling my first day's salary is going to be my last." Plucky Duck gulped.

And Plucky Duck was right. When he got back to the paper, Mr. Johnson fired him on the spot.

"Sorry, kid," Mr. Johnson said as he showed Plucky the door.

Skid! Skid!

Plucky took a copy of *The Acme Acres News* as he left the office. Maybe it would have an ad in it for another job.

He read the want ads from top to bottom. The most interesting job was at Mr. Guilliani's Pizza Parlor. Plucky Duck *loved* pizza.

That's for me! he thought.

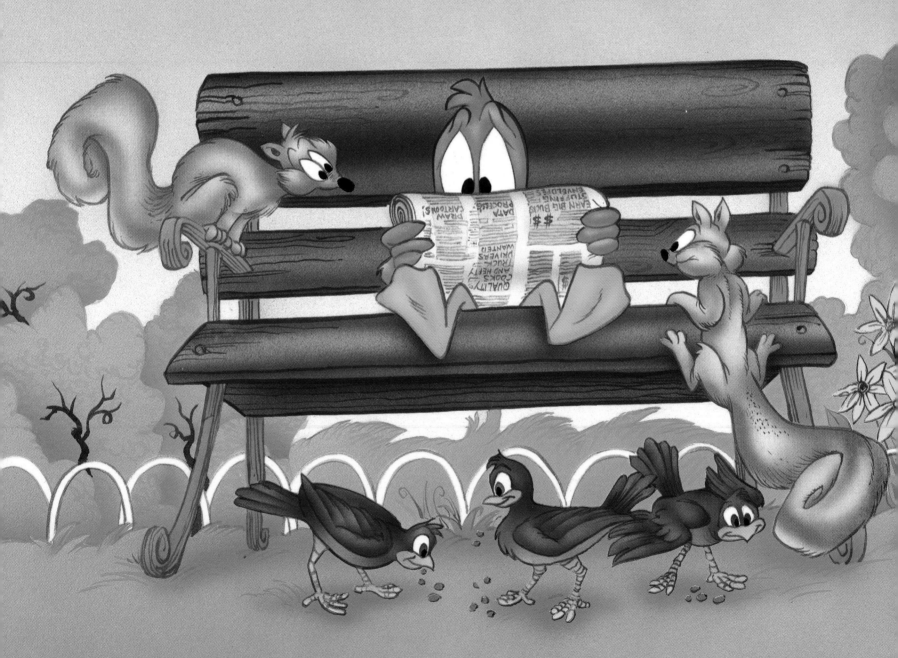

Mr. Guilliani hired Plucky Duck to help sweep out his pizza parlor and set the tables. Plucky was very impressed by the way Mr. Guilliani made pizza. He threw the dough all the way up in the air. Then he caught it.

Mr. Guilliani would be great on our football team, Plucky thought.

That afternoon, Buster, Babs, and Hamton stopped by for some pizza. Just at that moment, Mr. Guilliani got a telephone call.

"Plucky, tell the customers I'll be right back," Mr. Guilliani told him. "You can give them something to drink while they wait. And take their orders, too."

"So what would you like, guys?" Plucky Duck asked.

"One super giant pizza with everything on it," Babs Bunny ordered.

"Make that two," Hamton said.

That's when Plucky had his great idea. He had been watching Mr. Guilliani make pizza all morning. There was a lump of dough on the counter. He would start to make the pizza for Mr. Guilliani!

Plucky Duck tossed the dough high in the air. *Hey, this is easy!* he thought, catching it. He tossed it again.

That's when Mr. Guilliani came back. And that's when Plucky dropped the pizza dough.

Mr. Guilliani was not pleased.

"I'm sorry you lost the job, sport," Buster Bunny said as they left the pizza parlor.

"Oh, that's okay," Plucky replied. "There are other jobs. I wasn't making much *dough*, anyway!"

Plucky and Hamton were in the candy store that afternoon when they saw a notice on the bulletin board. It said, "Dog walker wanted for four adorable pooches."

"Hey. That's for you, Plucky," Hamton said.

Plucky went to the address on the card.

"These are our dogs," Mr. Brown told him. "Flopsy, Mopsy, Cottontail, and Peter. Say hello to Plucky Duck, you dear little pooches."

Mr. Brown turned to Plucky again. "They like to walk in the park for an hour or so. Why don't you take them out now?"

Wag! Wag!

So Plucky took the dogs out for a walk. But the dogs didn't like to walk—they liked to run. *This job is not easy*, Plucky Duck thought as the dogs dragged him down a path.

He tried as hard as he could to hold onto their leashes.

Suddenly, the dogs raced off the path, chasing a squirrel. Plucky ended up sitting in the middle of the path. The dogs danced around a nearby tree, barking. Plucky squinted. There, stuck in the ground, was something sparkly. It looked like some kind of ring.

Plucky pulled the ring out of the dirt and put it in his pocket. That's when his friends reached him.

"Gee, Plucky!" said Babs. "Are you okay?"

"I guess so," said Plucky.

By the time Plucky Duck had brushed himself off, all four dogs had disappeared.

"Oh, no," Plucky groaned. "Now I've lost Mr. Brown's dogs...and another job, too. I'd better go back and tell him."

"I'll go with you," Buster offered. "Me, too," said Babs. "And don't forget me!" Hamton called. So all four friends headed off to Mr. Brown's house to tell him about the missing dogs.

Plucky knocked on Mr. Brown's door. When Mr. Brown opened it, there were Flopsy, Mopsy, Cottontail, and Peter, barking happily.

"I'm surprised you came back," said Mr. Brown. "The dogs got here five minutes ago."

"I'm sorry," said Plucky. "I guess I'm fired."

Just then, Mrs. Brown walked into the room. She looked very unhappy.
"I'll never find my diamond ring, Horace. I just know it!" she wailed.
Plucky frowned. Then he reached into his pocket.
"Is this your ring?" he asked Mrs. Brown. "I found it in the park."

"Oh, it is! It is! Thank you, young man!" said Mrs. Brown. "I must have lost it when I took the pooches for their walk yesterday!"

"It was nothing," said Plucky, starting to walk out the door.

"Wait a minute," said Mr. Brown. "You can't leave without the reward."

"Reward?" asked Plucky.

"One hundred dollars," said Mr. Brown. "Here you are."

"This is terrific!" Plucky Duck shouted.

Mr. Brown smiled. "You know, Plucky," he said. "You were so honest about everything, you can still have the dog-walking job if you want it."

"Gee, Mr. Brown," said Plucky. "Thanks again. But now I don't *need* a job."

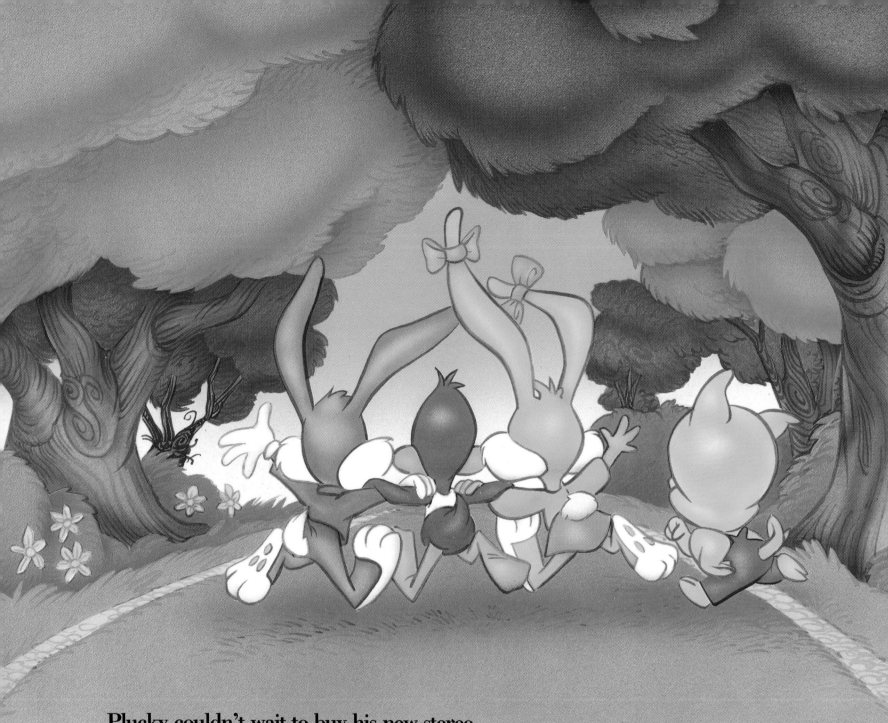

Plucky couldn't wait to buy his new stereo.

"Better make it a portable stereo, dude," Babs told him as they headed for Cousin Eddie's Electronics Emporium. "That way, you can bring it to the beach."

"Fer sure, Babs!" Plucky said happily. "Fer sure!"